Clovis Crawfish
and His Friends

THE CLOVIS CRAWFISH SERIES

(Pelican Publishing Company is reissuing the earlier titles with new color and black-and-white illustrations as the original editions go out of print.)

Mary Alice Fontenot

Clovis Crawfish and His Friends

Illustrated by Keith Graves

PELICAN PUBLISHING COMPANY
GRETNA 1985

For Ann Chopin and John Thistlethwaite
Marraine and *Parrain*
of Clovis Crawfish

Library of Congress Cataloging-in-Publication Data

Fontenot, Mary Alice.
   Clovis Crawfish and his friends.

   Summary: In the Louisiana Bayou Clovis Crawfish
tries to prevent M'sieu Blue Jay from making a meal
out of his friend Gaston Grasshopper.
   [1. Crayfish—Fiction. 2. Bayous—Fiction.
3. Louisiana—Fiction] I. Graves, Keith, ill.
II. Title.
PZ7.F73575Cle 1985   [E]   85-16994
ISBN 0-88289-479-X

Manufactured in the United States of America

Published by Pelican Publishing Company, Inc.
1101 Monroe Street, Gretna, Louisiana 70053

Foreword

In a few lively pages the gifted Mary Alice Fontenot has packed a wonderful love and understanding of the Louisiana scene, and a no less wonderful tale (as well as tail) of one of Louisiana's happiest of citizens and natural resources as well—the crawfish.

Clovis Crawfish and His Friends is a cheerful, zestful exploration of a distinguished native phenomenon, presented for the children of the state with spirit and skill and perception.

HARNETT T. KANE

Clovis Crawfish's real name was Clovis Clemence, but all his friends on the bayou called him Clovis. Clovis lived in a mud house on the bank of Bayou Queue de la Grenouille, which means Bayou Frog Tail in south Louisiana.

Clovis Crawfish wondered why the bayou was called Frog Tail because he knew that frogs don't have tails.

Bertile Butterfly flew by and lit on the honeysuckle vine.

"*Bonjour,* Bertile," said Clovis, which is the way to say "hello" in south Louisiana. "Do you know why our bayou is called Bayou Frog Tail?"

"Louisiana bayous have funny names," said Bertile as she flitted over the bayou. Bertile wasn't interested in anything except flowers.

Christophe Cricket crawled out from under the root of the big oak tree. He rubbed his wings together and chirped a happy song: "Be sweet! Be sweet!"

Clovis crawled around, wiggling his whiskers and holding up his big, sharp claws. His fan-shaped tail made little tracks in the soft mud on the bayou bank.

Just then a deep voice said, *"Ouaouaron! Ouaouaron!"*

Down at the edge of the water was Fernand Frog, the big bullfrog who lived in the bayou. Fernand jumped up on the bayou bank and blinked the water out of his big, round eyes.

"Fernand!" said Clovis. "You've lived in the bayou for a long, long time. Why is it called Bayou Frog Tail? Frogs don't have tails!"

"Of course frogs have tails!" said Fernand in his big, deep voice. "Didn't you know that?"

Clovis looked at Fernand. He crawled around and around Fernand and looked and looked, but he couldn't see any tail on Fernand.

"Are you sure you're a frog, Fernand?" said Clovis. "Because for sure you don't have a tail."

"Oh, I don't have it any more," said Fernand. "Baby frogs are born with tails to help them swim. But when they get to be big frogs like me, with big, strong legs to jump and swim with, they don't need the tails any more."

"*Mais jamais!*" said Clovis, which means "Never have I heard such a thing!" in Acadian-French.

Fernand jumped just to show Clovis how strong his back legs were. He jumped so high he went over the dewberry bush and landed in the bayou with a big splash. He swam away, his strong legs kicking out in the back like scissors opening and closing.

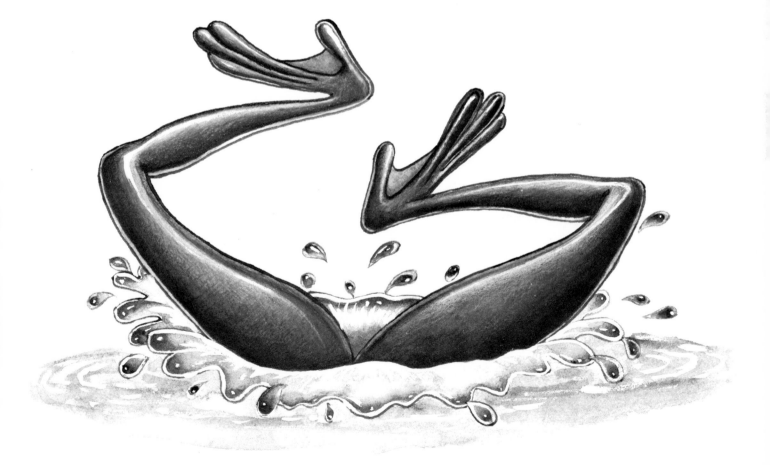

Clovis crawled down to the water and turned around. He backed off into the water, his fan-shaped tail snapping, and away he swam to the bottom of the bayou.

There was Clothilde Catfish, resting underneath a water lily, softly swishing her tail in the water. She waved to him with her whiskers, and Clovis waved back at her.

Theodore Turtle was taking a sun bath on top of an old log in the water. He stuck his head out of his shell long enough to say *"Bonjour"* as Clovis went by.

Comme Ci, Comme Ça

Music by Jeanne and Robert Gilmore

Com - ment ça va, mon a - mi, comment ça va. Comme-ci, comme

ça, cher pe - tit, comme-ci comme - ça.

Clovis crawled out on the bank again, and there was Gaston Grasshopper, sitting on a blade of grass.

"*Comment ça va, mon ami, comment ça va,*" said Gaston, which is the way to say, "How are you?" in south Louisiana.

"*Comme ci, comme ça, cher petit, comme ci, comme ça,*" said Clovis, which means, "I'm fine, little friend."

Gaston looked at Clovis's mud house. It had a hole in the middle and Gaston could see 'way, 'way down in the ground where Clovis had dug a deep hole with his big, sharp claws.

Denis Dirt Dauber flew down and lit on the wet mud near the water. He dug up some mud with his feet.

"I'm going to build a new house with this nice mud!" said Denis. "I need a big, big house for all the little dirt daubers I'm going to hatch!"

Maurice Mosquito Hawk lit on top of a thistle. Clovis could see the sun shining right through his wings. Maurice could see Clovis and Gaston and everything, all at the same time, because he has lots of eyes that can look up and down, backward and forward, and even sideways.

Lizette Lizard ran down the trunk of the big oak tree. When Lizette was on the tree trunk she was gray like the tree bark; when she ran onto the green grass she turned green.

Just then Clovis and his friends heard "CHANK-che-ANK! CHANK-che-ANK!"

"It's M'sieu Blue Jay!" said Gaston. "He wants to eat me!" And with one big jump down, he went into the hole in the middle of Clovis's mud house.

Lizette Lizard ran up the tree trunk and turned gray. Denis Dirt Dauber took off over the bayou with his load of wet mud. Maurice Mosquito Hawk was already out of sight.

"CHANK-che-ANK! CHANK-che-ANK!"
M'sieu Blue Jay perched on a branch of the big oak tree. He looked very hungry.

Clovis started backing down into the hole in the middle of his mud house. He didn't want M'sieu Blue Jay to eat his friend Gaston Grasshopper.

But old M'sieu Jay had a sharp eye. He just loved juicy grasshoppers, and he wasn't about to let Gaston get away. Down he flew, fast as a jet.

Clovis opened his claws wide, wide. M'sieu Jay swooped down again and pecked at Clovis.

M'sieu Jay flew down again, fast, fast. He grabbed Clovis in his sharp claw and flew up into the oak tree.

He put Clovis down on a wide limb, put his foot on him, and started pecking on Clovis's hard shell.

That made Clovis very mad. He pinched M'sieu Jay hard, hard, right through his feathers.

"CHANK-che-ANK! CHANK-che-ANK!"

M'sieu Jay was so surprised he almost fell off the tree limb.
He fluttered his wings and flew high up into the air, with Clovis
still pinching with his big left claw.

M'sieu Jay squawked and squawked, and he flew around
and around, but he couldn't make Clovis let go. He flew down on
the ground, then up into the tree again, whirling around and
squawking.

He flew around so fast and furiously that Clovis's claw broke off. Clovis fell to the ground, right in the middle of a patch of soft clover.

M'sieu Jay flew off across the bayou and into the woods, still with Clovis's big left claw pinched onto his feathers, and still squawking "CHANK-che-ANK!"

"You saved my life," said Gaston Grasshopper, "but you've lost your beautiful big left claw!"

Bertile Butterfly, Lizette Lizard, and Clothilde Catfish started to cry. Fernand Frog croaked, *"Ouaouaron!"* and cleared his throat. Maurice Mosquito Hawk and Denis Dirt Dauber sat on the thistle with their wings drooping. Theodore Turtle drew his head into his shell. Christophe Cricket stopped chirping.

Clovis didn't look at all worried. "Look!" he said to his friends. "I still have one claw, so I can fight for my friends and build mud houses too. And the claw that I lost will grow back. In just a while I'll have it back, big and strong as ever!"

Bertile Butterfly, Clothilde Catfish, and Lizette Lizard stopped crying. Theodore Turtle poked his head out of his shell. Maurice Mosquito Hawk and Denis Dirt Dauber flew away, their wings making happy, buzzing sounds.

Pronunciation Guide

French	Approximate Pronunciation	English
marraine	mah-rahn	godmother
parrain	pah-rahn	godfather
Clovis Clemence	klo-vees klay-mohns	Clovis Clemence
Bayou Queue de la Grenouille	bah-you kerr duh lah grin-oo-ee	Bayou Frog Tail
Bertile	bear-teel	Bertile
bonjour	baw-zhoor	good day (hello)
Christophe	krees-tawf	Christopher
ouaouaron	wah-wah-rohn	frog sound
Fernand	fehr-nahn	Ferdinand
mais jamais	meh zha-meh	never have I heard such a thing
Clothilde	klo-teel	Clothilde
Theodore	tay-o-dor	Theodore
Gaston	gass-tohn	Gaston
comment ça va	co-mohn sah vah	how are you
mon ami	mohn nah-mee	my friend
comme ci, comme ça	com see, com sah	I'm fine
cher petit	sheh puh-tee	dear little one
Denis	duh-nee	Dennis
Maurice	mo-rees	Morris
Lizette	lee-zet	Lizette
M'sieu	m-shuh	Mister